Sparky and Tidbit

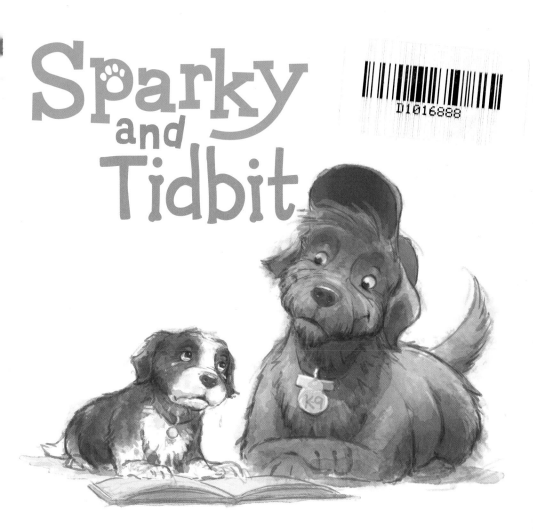

by Kathryn O. Galbraith

illustrated by Gerald Kelley

READY-TO-READ

Simon Spotlight

New York London Toronto Sydney New Delhi

Once again to Steve,
reader extraordinare
—K.O.G.

 SIMON SPOTLIGHT
An imprint of Simon & Schuster Children's Publishing Division
1230 Avenue of the Americas, New York, New York 10020
This Simon Spotlight edition February 2015
Text copyright © 2015 by Kathryn O. Galbraith
Illustrations copyright © 2015 by Gerald Kelley
SIMON SPOTLIGHT, READY-TO-READ, and colophon are registered trademarks of
Simon & Schuster, Inc.
For information about special discounts for bulk purchases, please contact Simon & Schuster
Special Sales at 1-866-506-1949 or business@simonandschuster.com.
The Simon & Schuster Speakers Bureau can bring authors to your live event. For more
information or to book an event contact the Simon & Schuster Speakers Bureau at 1-866-248-3049
or visit our website at www.simonspeakers.com.
Manufactured in the United States of America 1119 LAK
10 9 8 7 6 5 4 3 2
Library of Congress Cataloging-in-Publication Data
Galbraith, Kathryn Osebold.
Sparky and Tidbit / by Kathryn O. Galbraith ; illustrated by Gerald Kelley.
pages cm. — (Ready-to-read)
Summary: After receiving a K-9 badge for his birthday, Sparky is eager to prove himself a hero but
the only one he can find in trouble is Tidbit, a puppy who just needs help with his reading.
[1. Heroes—Fiction. 2. Literacy—Fiction. 3. Books and reading—Fiction 4. Dogs—Fiction.
5. Animals—Infancy—Fiction. 6. Schools—Fiction.] I. Kelley, Gerald, illustrator. II. Title.
PZ7.G1303Som 2015
[E]—dc23
2013050550
ISBN 978-1-4814-0425-9 (hc)
ISBN 978-1-4814-0424-2 (pbk)
ISBN 978-1-4814-0426-6 (eBook)

Table of Contents

Chapter 1:
Just Like a Hero

It was Sparky's birthday. On the table was a big box.

Happy Birthday!

Licks & Love from Uncle Spot

Sparky chewed right through the box in three big chomps. It was just what he wanted!

A K-9 cap. A K-9 collar. And a K-9 badge that sparkled in the sun.

He put the uniform right on. He looked brave and bold. Just like a hero. He was so impressed, he woofed. *Woof!*

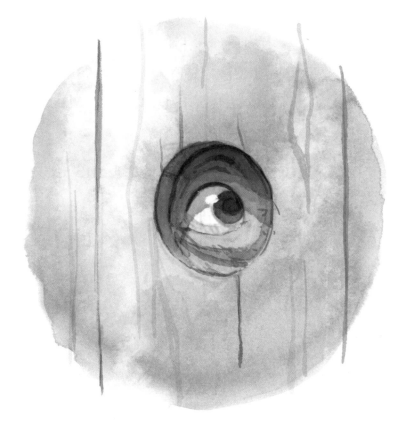

But to be a real hero, he needed to *do* something brave and bold. What would that be?

"I'll round up a gang of sneaky bone robbers," he decided.

Sparky crept under bushes. He peered through fences. He spied around trees.

There were no bone robbers anywhere. Not one. Sparky scratched his left ear.

"Hmm, what else would a real hero do?"

Sparky had another idea.

"I'll chase all the mean, hissy cats right out of town!"

Sparky trotted down the path, his new cap on his head, his new collar around his neck, and his new badge sparkling in the sun.

He spied old cats, black cats, striped cats and kittens. But no mean, hissy ones. Not one.

Sparky sighed. What else would a real hero do? Sparky had a bigger, better idea.

"I'll dig up buried treasure."

Sparky dug under the willow.

He dug near the rocks. He dug deep into Uncle Spot's garden patch. No treasures. Not one.

Sparky sighed again. He was running out of ideas.

"*Yip!*"

Sparky's short ears perked up. What was that? He cocked his head and listened.

"*YIP! YIP! YIP!*"

Hurray! It sounded like trouble!

Chapter 2:
Sparky to the Rescue!

"Wait!" Sparky barked. "I'll save you!"
He raced across the meadow.

This was his chance to do something brave and bold—something only a real hero could do.

As quick as a flea, Sparky discovered little Tidbit, a neighborhood pup, under a lilac bush with a book. Tears plip-plopped down his muzzle.

"What's the trouble, Tidbit?" he asked. "Sneaky bone robbers? Mean, hissy cats?"

"Nooooo!" Tidbit howled. "It's worse!"

Sparky sat back on his haunches. Worse! What could be worse than bone robbers or mean cats?

Now that he'd thought of it, he could think of several things. Cranky skunks. Pesky raccoons. Angry ducks.

He hoped it wasn't ducks. They always traveled in packs.

"Tidbit, speak!" Sparky barked quickly.

"Every . . . everyone in Little Pooch Puppy School can read better than I can," Tidbit whined.

Sparky couldn't believe his short ears. Tidbit didn't need saving after all. It was a wasted rescue!

"Oh, any pup can learn to read," Sparky told him.

Another tear trickled down Tidbit's muzzle.

"Not *this* pup," he whimpered.

Sparky hated to see Tidbit cry. But he still had hero work to do. He turned and . . .

"Oops!" He stepped on Tidbit's book.

"Richard the Red-Nosed Rabbit," he read. "I loved this story when I was a pup. It is so funny!"

Then he had an idea. "Hey, you can practice reading this to me."

"I can't." Tidbit began to sniffle. "It's the words! They are too hard. *Grrrrrr!* I hate them!"

Then he grabbed the book and bit it. Hard.

Chomp!

"No biting," Sparky barked.

He pointed to the spot right beside him.
"Sit."

Tidbit sat.

Sparky read the first sentence in the book.

"Now you try," he told Tidbit. "Go slowly,
and I'll just listen."

Tidbit grumbled under his breath, but
he obeyed. He read in a tiny whisper. He
sounded out every word.

"One . . . Once there was a ra-rab-bbit
named Rich . . . Richard. He had a red . . . "

Soon Sparky was sorry he'd ever thought of his idea. He tried not to yawn. He tried not to wiggle. Or waggle. Or scratch his ears. He tried not to think about all the hero work he wanted to do, but he thought about it anyway.

Finally Tidbit jumped up.

"Look! I did it! I read the *whole* page!"

Sparky sprang to his feet, too. "Good job!"

"Can we do it again tomorrow?" Tidbit watched him with eager eyes.

Sparky shook his head. "I'm too busy." Besides, sitting and listening was very hard work.

Tidbit began to sniffle. "Please, please, double please?"

"Well, okay," he answered. "But just *one* more time."

Chapter 3:
Practice, Practice, Practice

The next day Sparky met Tidbit near the lilac bush. Tidbit practiced his reading. He sounded out every word.

Sparky practiced his listening. He still wanted to yawn. And wiggle. And waggle. And scratch his ears. He still wanted to do his hero work. But he listened to every slow, whispered word.

It was a long afternoon.

Suddenly Tidbit barked, "I read the *whole* story all by myself!" He danced a happy pup dance right on the spot.

"Can you listen to me tomorrow?" he asked. "Please, please, please, triple please! Just one more time?"

Sparky shook his head. "I'm too busy."

Tidbit began to sniffle.

"Okay." Sparky sighed."But remember, just *one* more time."

The next day Tidbit brought a new book. *Three Mean Kittens Who Lost Their Socks.*

The words were a little bigger, a little harder. Tidbit read a little slower.

"Who wants to read about these silly puff balls?" he growled. He grabbed the book in his mouth and sent it flying.

Sparky didn't bark a word. Not one woof.

Tidbit waited. And waited.

Then he picked up the book again. "Oh, okay."

By the end of the week, Tidbit didn't stumble over any words.

"Three mean kittens lost their socks. And they began to hiss."

Tidbit looked up. "What silly puff balls."

But this time his tail wagged as he said it.

Chapter 4:
Ms. Beagle's Idea

Every afternoon Sparky met Tidbit under the lilac bush.

Every afternoon Tidbit's voice grew louder. Braver. Smoother.

Sparky was very pleased. Soon Tidbit would not need him at all. But not too soon, he hoped. He would really miss the stories. And Tidbit.

In school one Friday, it was Tidbit's turn in the Reading Circle.

He didn't trip over any words, not even the hard ones like *mail carrier*, *fire hydrant*, and *veterinarian*.

"Well done, Tidbit!" said his teacher, Ms. Dottie Beagle, and she gave him a bone. "You must have been practicing."

"Sparky helped me," Tidbit said. "He's a very good listener."

"Hmm, that gives me an idea." Ms. Beagle sat down at her desk. She pulled out a sheet of her official Little Pooch Puppy School paper.

Then she began to write.

Chapter 5:
The Official Listener

The next day Ms. Dottie Beagle's letter arrived in Sparky's mailbox.

Sparky was so surprised, he woofed. Twice. *Woof! Woof!*

This was only the second letter he'd ever received. The first one was from his dentist. He never answered that one.

Sparky quickly chewed through
the envelope.

Dear Sparky,

Will you please come
to my class today?
I have something important
to discuss with you.

Happy Bones,
Ms. Dottie Beagle

Sparky scratched his left ear. Then he scratched his right one.

Why did Ms. Beagle want to see *him*?

Uncle Spot always said to put your best feet forward. Sparky licked all four paws until they were neat and clean.

Then he put on his K-9 cap, his K-9 collar, and his sparkling K-9 badge.

Now he was ready to meet Ms. Beagle.

Sparky hurried to Tidbit's school.
Ms. Beagle was sitting at her desk.
"Sparky, I have a job for you."
"You do?" Sparky straightened
his K-9 cap. "Lost bones? Stolen balls?
Missing water bowls?"

Ms. Beagle shook her head.

"No, something more important. We would like you to be the Official Listener of the Little Pooch Puppy School."

Official Listener! Sparky's short ears perked up. His heart thumped.

Ms. Beagle pointed. "And there is your Official Listening Den."

The floor was covered with a grass green rug. There were pillows and piles of books everywhere.

"There's *Good Night Bone!*" he barked. "And here is *Pups with Frog and Toad.*"

Ms. Beagle waved her tail.

"Speak, Sparky. I hope you will join us."

Chapter 6:
Tidbit's Story

Sparky couldn't speak.

He was too excited.

But he nodded his head until his K-9 cap slipped over his eyes.

Sparky started his new job that very day. One by one, young pups came to read to him.

Sometimes they read in tiny whispers.

Sometimes they stumbled over new words like *kibble* and *collar* and had to sound them out.

Sometimes they just sat and showed Sparky the pictures.

But they all loved sitting against
his warm, broad back.

And Sparky?

He never yawned. He never wiggled
Or waggled. Or scratched his ears.

He sat very still and listened—with his
heart as well as his ears.

One morning Sparky trotted into the classroom and . . .

"Surprise!"

"Welcome to Story Day!" Ms. Beagle howled. "Every pup has written one to share. Who wants to go first?"

"Me!"

"Me!"

Eighteen paws shot up.

Ms. Beagle nodded to Tidbit.

Tidbit scampered to the front of the room. "Once there was a dog named Sparky," he read. His voice was loud and strong.

The pups quieted down. Sparky's short ears perked up. A story about him! His tail perked up too.

"Every day I read to him near the lilac bush.

He didn't yawn if I was slow.

He didn't bark when I messed up.

And he never, ever growled.

He listened no matter what.

When I'm a big dog,

I want to be just like Sparky.

He is my hero!

The end."

All the pups yapped and barked.
And Sparky?
He did what he did best. He sat
very still and listened.
Then he jumped up and . . .

. . . took a big bow-WOW!